Last Train Home

A play by Brent Winzek

Space Cadets Studios

Edited by Zachary Gold

Cover Art by Monica Kay

DEDICATION

To the Professors Chambers, who revealed for me the abstract side of theater and challenged me to hone my craft.

ACKNOWLEDGMENTS

This publication would not be material without the efforts and encouragement of editor, cohort, and friend Zack Gold. It would not have its current shape or structure without astute feedback from playwright, performer, and friend Sean T. McGrath. Further edits would not have been possible without the keen eyes of test reader Tracy Winzek. And this play simply would not have been penned if my wife, Monica, hadn't tolerated all my strange writing habits from the very start.

PERFORMANCE RIGHTS

CONCEPTUAL STATEMENT

"Hell is other people." Sartre's quote perfectly captures the feeling I had every time I clamored down the steps at 181st Street in Washington Heights to catch the subway back in 2015. I was in my mid-twenties and already facing a divorce. Trekking through those tubes in an emotionally volatile state – being an exposed nerve in a storm of humanity – was like descending into Hell in Dante's wake. Down I'd go, and so too would my spirits, tumbling down the rabbit hole.

My only distraction was the action around me. As a result, many of the characters and monologues represented in this piece are inspired by very real notes I took on very real humans residing in the cracks and crevices of dear old Manhattan. I thank them for their distractions and enclose their brilliant whimsy herein for others to enjoy. As Shakespeare so famously observed, "All the world's a stage, and all the men and women merely players."

CONTENTS

CAST

JOSIE – F

OLIVER/THOMAS – M

HELEN/FIREFIGHTER – F

WIZARD/PASTOR/ROACH 1 – M or NB

INGRID/ROACH 2 – F

CRACK ADDICT/UNCLE BOB/ROACH 3 – M

CONDUCTOR/OMAR/MOLE PERSON 1 – M or NB

CANDI/LAUGH. GIRL/MOLE PERSON 2 – F or NB

BOXERS 1 & 2 can be assigned to anyone above.

MOLE PERSONs 3 & 4 can be assigned to anyone above.

PRODUCTION NOTES

CASTING:

These roles are intended for a diverse cast. While the ideal role breakdown is included, divide roles in any way necessary, except for Oliver/Thomas and Helen/Firefighter.

There should be at least four (4) Mole People in total, including Mole Persons 1 & 2.

For nonbinary casting, change pronouns as needed.

STAGE DIRECTIONS:

Many of the stage directions within the script suggest spectacle and may therefore seem outlandish or impractical. The creative team need only capture their essence.

SCENE 1

A New York City subway car. Present day.

The car doors open with a ding and JOSIE *gets on the train. She sits down near* HELEN, *an older lady.*

The subway pulls out of the station, and the two passengers sit in silence.

Josie produces an envelope and pulls a two-page handwritten letter from it. She does not open the letter, just plays with the edges.

The subway lurches. The brakes squeal.

CONDUCTOR: (*over train speakers*) Attention, ladies and gentlemen. We are being held momentarily by the train's dispatcher. We apologize for any inconvenience.

OLIVER, *a quirky, middle-aged man wearing a purple bow tie, enters their car through the rear door. He leans into a seat, reading the names carved into the plastic interior.*

Josie and Helen stare at him as he approaches their seats. He leans in close, squinting at a carving very near to Josie's face.

OLIVER: Excuse me. Sorry. (*he puts on his reading glasses*) That one there! Do you mind reading it to me? What does it say?

JOSIE: What?

1

OLIVER: Oh, pardon me. I must sound like a lunatic. These are old reading glasses, not my normal ones. I'm looking for a message carved in one of these seats. That inscription there. Carved into the seat. Do you mind reading that to me?

Helen sits up, eyeing Oliver like a hawk.

Josie feigns ignorance for a moment before realizing she's cornered.

JOSIE: Oh, uh... 'Steve was here.'

OLIVER: Damn. What about underneath it there?

JOSIE: 'Steve's a twat.'

Oliver scoffs, then mumbles to himself as he walks away, peering at the other subway seats as he wanders.

JOSIE: (*calling after him*) Excuse me? What are you doing?

OLIVER: I'm looking for a heart. (*snickers*) I sound like the Tinman. That's funny. I'm sorry – I swear I'm a normal person. Normal-ish. It's just – I'm looking for a heart with initials carved into it.

JOSIE: What initials?

OLIVER: O. T. That's Oliver Thomas. That's me.

JOSIE: Oh, funny.

OLIVER: Why?

JOSIE: My hu – uh – I know a guy named Thomas Oliver.

OLIVER: How 'bout that?

JOSIE: So, Oliver: is there anything special about your engraving?

OLIVER: It's in a heart with a girl's initials.

JOSIE: What's her name?

OLIVER: I can't remember. That's not the important part. I know they didn't just get rid of that train car.

HELEN: How long ago was it?

OLIVER: Oh, at least twenty years now.

HELEN: They got rid of that car.

OLIVER: Well, I haven't checked every car yet. So, I don't know. But I will soon. And I know they didn't get rid of that car.

JOSIE: How can you be sure? I bet they get rid of cars all the time.

OLIVER: No way. It was brand new back when I did that. In its prime! Look at some of these old cars: They've been plugging along these tracks for forty years or more, a lot of them. And my car- it's still going... whispering a love story to anyone who reads the initials and wonders about it. I just want to sit with it for a while. Try to take it all in again. Remember her name. I can remember her smell. Her hair and her laugh. But she's nameless. I never thought I'd do that. We carved out a place – that place – here on a train car. A little place in time. A way to be remembered by strangers.

JOSIE: Why does it matter so much?

OLIVER: It doesn't, truthfully. But that was our legacy. I need to recall her name. I owe her that much.

JOSIE: If you don't remember, she can't mean that much. You're building it up in your head.

OLIVER: I don't see it that way. We shared something. In retrospect, it was very brief, I guess. If I'm being honest. But we did have a connection. For a while. We were intimate and we held each other. A human connection. Wouldn't you want to know her name – or his name?

JOSIE: I'm trying to forget.

OLIVER: A boy?

JOSIE: Uh... yes. A boy. A husband, actually.

OLIVER: (*taking a seat next to Josie*) You're married?

JOSIE: Legally.

OLIVER: But you're so young!

JOSIE: Yeah. I get that a lot.

HELEN: (*under them*) She isn't that young.

OLIVER: Apologies.

HELEN: (*under them*) I almost married at nineteen. She looks twenty-five, at least.

JOSIE: Honestly not sure why I said anything. You remind me of what he'll probably be like when he's older.

OLIVER: Oh, I see. If it helps, you can talk to me.

JOSIE: No offense, but I don't know you.

4

OLIVER: But when I find my initials, then you'll know me. You'll remember me. A physical imprint- a ghost on the subway... Maybe you told me because you don't know me? There's power to be found in that. People imprint on each other. Maybe you need to talk about him: this person you're trying to forget.

JOSIE: I really don't.

OLIVER: You told a total stranger.

HELEN: He's got you there.

JOSIE: I made a mistake. I don't want to talk about it, especially right before I see him—

OLIVER: You're going to see him?

Realizing what she's done, Josie hangs her head.

JOSIE: Yeah.

OLIVER: That means you don't live together anymore.

JOSIE: Please stop.

The subway car shudders; the lights flicker. Metal brakes squeal and the train car tilts forty-five degrees, jerks to a halt, and the three passengers are jolted from their seats.

Josie struggles to her feet, holding her forehead.

OLIVER: Whoa! Okay! Okay? Are you okay?

JOSIE: I'm fine. I'll be fine. Just hit my head. I'm fine.

OLIVER: Easy. Easy. Don't get up so fast.

Oliver helps Josie sit, then sees that Helen is slumped over in her seat.

OLIVER: Ma'am, how about you? Ma'am? Oh, no.

As Oliver sits next to Helen and gently tries to revive her, the loudspeaker crackles.

CONDUCTOR: Attention ladies and gentlemen: we are experiencing minor delays on this line due to a train derailment. We should be moving shortly. Please remain in your car unless instructed otherwise by an MTA employee or police officer. We apologize for any inconvenience. Thank you for riding with MTA – New York City transit.

JOSIE: God, it's always something. How long will that take to fix?

OLIVER: Did they say the train derailed?

JOSIE: Yeah, they did.

OLIVER: I've never experienced that before. Not sure how long it could take, but we won't be moving shortly, that's for sure. And y'know, I've been on trains that sit in the station because of a sick passenger, and that takes them forever to orchestrate. I mean, how hard can it be to move someone off the train and onto a bench? (*shaking his head*) We've got to get a doctor or someone. It looks like she hit her head.

JOSIE: I'll find someone.

Josie rushes across the train car to the conductor's box. She knocks on the door, but no one answers. She tests the door handle. It's locked.

While Josie's back is turned, Helen sits upright. Oliver sits, scratching his head. He doesn't seem to notice her.

HELEN: Am I dead?

JOSIE: Did she just talk?

OLIVER: No. Look at her! She's out cold.

HELEN: Does that mean I'm dead?

JOSIE: No… Do you feel dead?

HELEN: Oh, shit.

JOSIE: I'm sorry.

HELEN: I felt like today was a good day.

JOSIE: It still is. It still can be.

HELEN: It's fine. It still is a good day. I mean… you know… to die.

JOSIE: What? When is it ever a good day to die?

HELEN: It was pretty. A pretty fall day. With the sunlight falling in spackled patches on the sidewalk. And it wasn't too cold. Did you notice?

JOSIE: Can't say I did.

HELEN: Oh. Well, I did. (*beat*) I sat on a bench for thirty- nine minutes. Just by myself. Just to be outside. I walk up and down West Seventieth Street every day, and I just sat on a bench and took it in. For the first time in, oh, I couldn't say. Twenty-some odd years? I miss my husband. I've forgotten his name… Harold? Yes, that sounds right. That must be it. How foolish that I can't remember. You know, it's funny; I really felt alive today. It would be a decent day. A decent note to end on.

JOSIE: Don't you have loved ones here?

HELEN: Oh, sure. No direct family. Just my sister. Half-sister. My older half-sister. My Harold was sterile, you see. So, we just adopted my sister's family. My half-sister. Older half-sister. But they're a bit... lower class, so it was always interesting taking them out in public. I just miss Harold. We used to travel. He always had business in Phoenix. We'd be out there at least three times a year. Have you ever been to Phoenix?

JOSIE: No. No, I haven't.

HELEN: You should go. It's at the north end of this train. The front of the train, just down the rabbit hole. (*she stops, confused at her own words*) It's in Arizona, Phoenix is. But you should go to the front of the train. Go down the tunnel to the front of the train. (*still confused*) I'm sorry. I don't know where that's coming from–

She goes limp again as a train CONDUCTOR *opens the door between cars. Josie watches as Oliver moves for the first time since Helen spoke. He tries to gently pat her cheek as the conductor rushes up.*

CONDUCTOR: Awe, shit. What the hell's going on?

OLIVER: We've got an injured lady here.

CONDUCTOR: Injured?

OLIVER: She's breathing, but we can't wake her up. She needs help.

CONDUCTOR: I played the announcement! Geez! What else do you want from me? We need a doctor! Someone in here a doctor?

OLIVER: There's only the three of us in this car. Don't you have a first aid kit? Smelling salts or something?

CONDUCTOR: I'm a conductor, not a doctor, damn it! Why would I ask for a doctor if I was one? Why would I be here on the train if I was a doctor? Wearing a uniform and pretending to be a conductor?

The Conductor and Oliver freeze again, and Helen sighs heavily. Josie looks to her, but as she does, Oliver re-animates next to her, snatches the letter held loosely in Josie's hand, and bolts for the front of the train.

JOSIE: Hey!

She starts after him, but Helen's pleas stop her.

HELEN: Wait! Don't leave. I'm alone here–

JOSIE: I'm here with you. I can hear you–

HELEN: But you're just strangers. All of you. Just blank faces with no obligation to me. Should I need help, that is. But I don't. I am an island. I'm not sure what that means. I was once a beautiful little patch of sand in a chain of reefs and barrier islands, like the ones dotting the Caribbean. But the older I get, the more I realize life has washed over those other islands. One by one. Slowly. Painfully. Hurricanes and high tides sucked them back into the sea, and I stand alone. No man is an island? That's because women outlive them. People abandon each other in the end. It's not their fault – not anybody's fault – it's just the way life built us. We weren't put together with time

HELEN (cont.): in the equation. (*she finally locks eyes with Josie*) This is the last train home. Get to the front of the train. Get your letter back. You'll try to convince yourself that you have other options, but you don't. Go down the tunnel and don't look back.

Helen falls limp or she disappears completely, swallowed by the train. Josie shakes her head and blinks.

JOSIE: What?

The Conductor does not move. He doesn't even breathe.

Josie watches him as she edges her way to the door at the end of the car.

As she grabs the handle, the Conductor moves again.

The lights flicker, and mechanical hissing and clanking roars within the train car.

Josie flings the door open and brilliant light bursts through the doorway followed by an immediate BLACKOUT.

SCENE 2

Josie slips into the second train car, forcing the door shut behind her.

This startles the WIZARD: *a thin, tall man hunched over in a corner seat.*

The Wizard's age is ambiguous. He is a man-child. It's unclear if he's just a backwards seventeen-year-old with an intense imagination, or a thirty-six-year-old man with a severe case of baby face.

He wears a Wizard's hat covered in silver suns and moons, thick horn-rimmed glasses, a grey strap-on beard, a green cloak, and his Wizard robe is unmistakably a reappropriated dress. His generic sneakers and bagged out tube socks are as dirty as his thick glasses.

He holds a wooden staff in one hand and his other is hidden inside a frightfully cute DRAGON *puppet. Both the Wizard and his Dragon (voiced by the Wizard) sound like a child's Sean Connery impersonation.*

In a corner somewhere, the LAUGHING GIRL *sits quietly, in her own world, laughing silently to herself. She is a plain-looking girl with wild hair. While the other characters in the train car will not acknowledge her, she can react to what they are doing and saying.*

As Josie spins around, holding the door closed, the Wizard jumps to his feet. He does not look at Josie, but his Dragon turns to her.

DRAGON: And what have we here?

JOSIE: Oh. Sorry. I didn't mean to disturb you.

DRAGON: Yet you have!

JOSIE: I'm sorry.

DRAGON: What is it you're running from? What's on the other side of that door?

JOSIE: A completely irrational conductor who doesn't want me to get where I'm going.

Throughout this introductory exchange, Josie is more concerned with the door than the Wizard and his Dragon. She continues to peer through the dirty glass window in the door.

DRAGON: Irrational? Such a big word for such a small person!

JOSIE: Uh...

DRAGON: Do ya' like big words?

JOSIE: I – uh – never really thought about it.

DRAGON: Well, my master, the grand Wizard, loves a nice big word. Tell us one.

JOSIE: What?

DRAGON: Tell us a nice big word. We like to hear them.

JOSIE: I'm sorry. I'm a little preoccupied right now.

DRAGON: Well, tell us a big word and we'll help you.

JOSIE: How?

DRAGON: My master will cast a spell and lock that door. No pesky conductors. Just us. Just the three of us, sitting here intimately. Sharing big words.

JOSIE: That's okay. I think I'll just hold it shut.

DRAGON: Don't be foolish!

JOSIE: I'm not. I like my chances better if I'm just holding the door shut. Thanks.

DRAGON: Do you doubt the Subway Wizard's sorcery?

JOSIE: Yes. Absolutely.

The Wizard turns to face her, striking a pose with his staff, taking a wide stance.

WIZARD: Stand back, doubter!

Josie tries to ignore him.

WIZARD: M'lady, I said stand back!

Thunder and lightning shake the train car, and the Wizard's voice rumbles, amplified by some ethereal force.

WIZARD: Defy me again and you receive no aid! I command you: stand away from that door!

Frightened, Josie dives into the seat next to the door and shields her face with her hands as the Wizard swings his staff. This grandiose gesture builds, threatening to climax in some extreme spectacle. Instead, as the Wizard finally points his staff at the door, it simply clicks.

The thunder and lightning subside, and the Wizard lowers his staff.

Hearing the cacophony subside, Josie peeks out from behind her hands.

WIZARD: Ah. There. Now, madam, let us hear some big, fancy words.

JOSIE: Ambivalent.

WIZARD: Oh, my! Yes! (*tasting the word in his mouth*) Ambivalent. Another!

JOSIE: Entrepreneurial?

WIZARD: Six syllables! Oh, you're good. You are good. Splendid job. I'd like to keep you around.

JOSIE: I have to get out. I'm going to the front of the train.

WIZARD: No. You must stay here. Please? I'm not afraid to tell you that we're a little frightened.

DRAGON: Yes. We're frightened. But not afraid to admit it. We'll admit it.

JOSIE: Yeah. You just did.

DRAGON: So, we did!

WIZARD: So, we did!

JOSIE: I'm sorry I can't stay. You can come with me if you want. So that you're not afraid.

WIZARD: No. It would be unwise to move. We should stay put. When you lose something, start looking for it where you last saw it.

DRAGON: That's what they'll do with our train. They'll start looking where they lost us.

JOSIE: I'm not waiting for them to come around.

DRAGON: A foolish choice. But yours to make.

JOSIE: It's okay to be frightened. But you should do something about it.

Josie steps politely past the Wizard, nodding to both the dragon and him. As she grabs the door handle to slide it open, the Wizard holds both hands up in surrender.

WIZARD: Wait!

JOSIE: Yes?

WIZARD: If we accompany you, will you share more big, confusing words with us?

DRAGON: To ease our fears?

JOSIE: If you get scared, ask for a word. But let's get going.

DRAGON: Could we have a word before you open the door?

JOSIE: Come to the door first.

The Wizard abides, batting puppy-dog eyes at Josie.

JOSIE: Reciprocal.

WIZARD: You are a true magician!

Someone bangs on the door at the other end of the train, back where Josie entered.

The lights flicker, and mechanical hissing and clanking roars within the train car once again.

Josie slides the door open and pulls the Wizard through with her.

BLACKOUT.

SCENE 3

Josie rushes into the third train car, followed by the Wizard.

In the middle of the car sits INGRID, a powerful woman. She lounges on a grassy knoll at the far end of the train car, blocking the door. Her dress is made of tree bark and birds nest in her hair.

She fans herself as she mumbles.

INGRID: It's always so hot on these fucking trains. In winter, in summer – doesn't matter. Who do they think is riding these blessed things? Everyone has a coat and a scarf on, it's a brisk forty-five degrees out. Just enough to make you sweat if you're really movin' through a crowd, and the operators or whoever runs these things, they crank that warm, suffocating heat until you sweat like a hog just sitting there in your chair. And Lord, do I sweat in the summer too, now.

WIZARD: Mother?

INGRID: I'm not your mother, child.

DRAGON: You look like his mother. Strikingly so.

INGRID: I only have one baby boy, and you ain't him. He's a big boy. With some consistency, you understand?

JOSIE: Excuse me, can we get past?

WIZARD: Can we stay with you?

JOSIE: What? No–

INGRID: So damn hot today. You know, I wear as little as possible. I'm a bigger woman, so I try and be modest, but oh my, my. Grueling. My baby teases me, says it's swamp ass. I don't know about all that, and forgive the dirty language, but I do sweat like no other, and it's fucking uncomfortable. It's such a pain getting nice for work. If I could afford it, I'd buy a car and sit in the traffic instead. At least there I'd have control of the temperature. But I'm rambling. And none of us really has control, do we? If you're lucky, God does.

JOSIE: I don't believe in God.

INGRID: Oh my! Why, child?

JOSIE: It's a long story.

INGRID: You used to, though?

JOSIE: Yeah.

INGRID: You wanna' talk about it with old Ingrid? I'm a good listener.

JOSIE: No, thanks. I'd really just like to pass by.

WIZARD: But we will stay!

JOSIE: I thought you were coming with me?

DRAGON: So did we. But we'd like to stay and talk with old Ingrid.

INGRID: Pipe down. You can all three stay, if you like. But you two – (*she points to the Wizard & his Dragon*) – need to be quiet for just a minute

INGRID (cont.): or two. (*focusing on Josie*) You've been hurt. (*Josie shrugs, about to answer, but Ingrid continues.*) I can see it in your eyes. That's okay. You'll find your way back.

JOSIE: I'd really like to just keep moving. I have to get to the front of the train.

INGRID: Why?

JOSIE: My note. A man named Oliver stole my note and he's taking it to the front of the train.

INGRID: Why?

JOSIE: I don't know. He just grabbed it from me and took off. But I need it. It has all my answers.

INGRID: Answers to what?

JOSIE: I wrote the answers to questions he asked me about our future. I don't remember what I wrote down. It's all hazy in my head, and I'm not sure if that's because I wrote it on a rainy day or if it's all slipping away. It rains a lot more these days, doesn't it?

INGRID: Sit down, I insist you sit with me and talk. We're not supposed to switch cars anyway.

JOSIE: I know, but I need my answers.

INGRID: You already know the answers, dear. The front of the train won't get you any closer. Besides, it's not about the destination, it's about the journey.

JOSIE: I don't think that really applies here.

INGRID: You have the answers already.

JOSIE: Ah.

INGRID: Care to know how?

JOSIE: No. I just want to pass through.

INGRID: Tell me how you were hurt. I'll even share my
    biscuits with you. Here.

*She produces a plate of pocket watches topped with cheese from
within the grassy mound.*

JOSIE: Is there any other way you'd let me pass?

INGRID: No.

JOSIE: I'd really rather not.

INGRID: I know. That's why I want to know so bad.
    I'm not gonna tell anyone. I'm harmless.
    Harmless Ingrid. That's what you can call me.

JOSIE: I'm supposed to decide whether or not I want a
    divorce.

INGRID: Oh, my! You married?

JOSIE: Yes.

INGRID: But you're so young!

JOSIE: So I've been told.

INGRID: Have you decided what you want?

JOSIE: No... How long am I going to have to talk about
    this?

INGRID: Until I'm done.

JOSIE: That's unfair.

INGRID: Relax. The train's derailed. You've got
    nowhere to be in a hurry. Where were you going?

JOSIE: To meet...

INGRID: Him?

JOSIE: Yes.

INGRID: Don't be uncomfortable. Sit. Sit. Have a biscuit. Please, I insist. Would you like something to drink?

WIZARD: We would, please!

INGRID: Hush. Or I won't let you stay. Sweetie, do you want a cup of tea?

Ingrid digs in a shopping bag and fishes out a piping hot tea kettle.

JOSIE: No, thank you. I'm more of a coffee person.

INGRID: Well, I don't have any of that. I don't have the stomach for it. Never have. It's too acidic, and my whole family suffers from acid reflux. Well, nearly everyone. My father had terrible heartburn, but I have a hunch that was also acid reflux. Common mistake, you know. Tea, though. Tea's good for your stomach. And warm beverages, they loosen the bowels. I always thought coffee created a double whammy that way. Because coffee is a warm beverage, but it's also an antioxidant. That means it loosens your bowels twice as much. No one wants to be that regular.

JOSIE: When you put it that way...

INGRID: What do you do for a living?

JOSIE: Not sure yet.

INGRID: That doesn't make sense at all.

JOSIE: I've done a couple different things. I'm just not sure what I want to do yet, that's all.

INGRID: Don't get defensive. Most people your age are doing nothing but working. Even if they've chosen a hopeless field. My boy wanted to be an actor. I told him absolutely not. He's not the most artistic, you see, but I dated an actor when I was young. I've seen that lifestyle. It's no way to live. Not in this city. What do you do?

JOSIE: I'm sort of a musician. But I do a lot of temp work.

INGRID: Oh, so you're an artistic type, too.

JOSIE: Not really.

INGRID: Don't deny it. I can tell by the way you're dressed. Very Bohemian. I know. I dated an actor when I was younger. I lived with him for a little bit after I was evicted from my own place. You know he didn't even have a bed frame? Just a mattress plopped on the floor and a couple of old movie posters. One was Shaft. Isaac Hayes, mind you. The original Shaft. The real Shaft. That was when I dabbled with witchcraft. Don't be afraid though, I'm a Christian woman now. Have you ever tried a Pagan religion?

JOSIE: What? No.

INGRID: I recommend a three-year trial period in your late twenties.

JOSIE: Oh. Probably not something I'll try.

INGRID: I'm sorry, are you judging me? I'm not judging you. Don't you worry. I just love others as best I

INGRID (cont.): can. That's right. And it shocks other people when I tell them that. I have all types of friends. I like shocking the people at church. Cooped up in their outdated beliefs. But Jesus, he spent time with prostitutes and sickly types. Not the likes of these people who have good lives and no real worries. People who spend all their time in those fancy offices, they don't understand the cogs in the machine, even if they spent their whole life in this city. They're used to the pecking order. They can go right to Hell, though. And I'd gladly tell them that.

JOSIE: Do you think I could pass through now?

INGRID: Just a second. I'm almost done with you.

A CRACK ADDICT *enters the car from the ceiling, or through a secret compartment in the floor. He carries a bouquet of flowers, and wears a shirt and tie, but with cycling shorts and a matching helmet. His feet are bare, and they look like the spindly digits of an iguana. He clambers in and stands between Josie and Ingrid.*

CRACK ADDICT: Excuse me. May I have your attention please. Excuse me. I hate to disrupt your ride, but I am homeless. I am not out on the streets trying to steal from people, I'm not here lying about what I need money for. I need food. Or a job. I'm doing my best to look good, and I am interested in doing an interview right away with anyone who wants to consider giving me work. I'm an honest man. Does anyone please have some food for me or work? Any spare change. Anything at all? Even a prayer?

INGRID: Here, have a sandwich. (*produces one from her bag*) Please. And Lord, I pray you help this man find a means to support himself. Please nourish him in the meantime with this sandwich.

CRACK ADDICT: Bless your heart, ma'am. Thank you kindly.

INGRID: It's real good. My favorite. Honey mustard, tomato, mozzarella, and glazed chard. Very healthy.

CRACK ADDICT: Thank you. Bless you. Thank you.

The Crack Addict unwraps the sandwich, eating it with precision. After a moment, he plucks the tomato from it and drops it on the floor.

Ingrid shoots Josie a look, then watches as the Crack Addict methodically plucks out the chard and wipes it off on Ingrid's mound.

INGRID: I'm sorry. Is the food not to your liking?

CRACK ADDICT: It's got all this slimy stuff on it. Slimy stuff's bad for my complexion. I'm hoping to get a modeling job for the magazines. That's what I'm hoping for. That's where the money is. Or in finance. I used to do all my own finances.

INGRID: Beggars can't be choosers. That's a perfectly nourishing sandwich and you just plucked out the most important bits.

He ignores her, his attention fixed on Josie now. He saunters over to her, still picking apart the sandwich, taking a bite here and there as he talks.

23

CRACK ADDICT: My tooth aches. Y'know when you've got that itch in your mouth, just above the jaw? It's like a loose filling nattering at my brain. It clouds me over and blocks my vision, and I trudge on through the fog. You ever grope like that? Like you're out in some field and you can't find your dentist's office 'cause he's out in some God-awful town in the flat, ugly parts of the Midwest? The heartland. That's what they call it. And people say – they tell me I'm throwing away my life out here. In the concrete jungle. That's what they call it. Living out here on this stuff. But how 'bout them, huh? Not sayin' they don't make a decent living, but I've just never understood monotony. Routine. I wanna' wake up at eight pee-em on a snowy January and reach the stars; stand in a field under the heavens. That's what the universe is. It's heaven. People say heaven's in the clouds, but it's not. I once carved the words 'I love you' into four feet of snow out in a field. Heartbroken and sad. Helpless and lost because I'd just been let go. And I tell you, that moment made me feel closer to God than I ever have. Out at night, without a soul around. That's when it happens. Under the stars- the heavens. I want that life. Driven by love and experiences that force us to our ends. The toothache. 'cause when your tooth aches, you know you need more blow! (*he cackles, nudging Josie*) But really. That toothache means I'm still alive. And I'm not pissing it away worried about money and a routine. See, that's hard work. It's hard work doing nothing. But we forget. You don't know what it's like to fight for your life. To have it and

CRACK ADDICT (cont.): be well and not lose it in that vast, eventless expanse we call routine or career or a living. Out there in the Midwest. In suburbia somewhere. California. Or Tennessee. Idaho. You ever been to Idaho?

JOSIE: (*dismissive*) I know – well, knew – some people out there.

CRACK ADDICT: Phew! So, you know what I mean. I been able to see about forty-two of our congruent states, and there are some beautiful places, but they're all ruined by people. That's what the travel ads never tell you. Populations just setting up shop and doing nothing. I just want to float on. Float on and fight on. For my life. Because that's truly living. To me.

JOSIE: Sure.

CRACK ADDICT: There is no universal truth. You remember that.

JOSIE: Okay.

CRACK ADDICT: Hey... you got any blow?

JOSIE: No. Sorry. I'm fresh out.

CRACK ADDICT: Yeah, sure. Whatever, man. That's cold. You remember that when you try to sleep tonight.

The Crack Addict staggers off into darkness.

Ingrid shakes her head.

INGRID: (*quietly*) You sleep just fine tonight. Don't think a thing of him. That right there is why I get frustrated trying to do the right thing. That was

INGRID (cont.): my best sandwich, you know. Lying there on the floor in a heap of slop because he thought it was slimy.

JOSIE: I've got to go. Come with me? Buddy system?

INGRID: Aren't you sweet?

WIZARD: No!

DRAGON: Stay!

The Wizard sits at the base of Ingrid's knoll, hugging it. He stays there with his Dragon, watching everything play out around him.

INGRID: I'm sitting right here so I can be found. Just like my grandma always told me. She'd say, "You get lost, child, you'd better just stay put. Where you got lost is where they'll all start looking to find you."

JOSIE: You'll let me past?

INGRID: You're your own person. Just be safe.

JOSIE: Thanks.

Josie climbs over the mound and rushes to the other end of the car. She heaves the door open. As she steps out, we see her slip, falling down between the cars.

INGRID: (*up to the heavens*) I tried. You saw me try.

BLACKOUT.

SCENE 4

Josie tumbles to the edge of the stage, stopped there by a sea of fleshy-looking rocks. They jiggle like muscles when touched.

As she stands, her head bumps against the limp bodies of plucked chickens hanging from the ceiling of the train tunnel. She looks upstage, in the direction of the subway cars.

Behind her, OMAR THE VETERAN *zips in on his motorized wheelchair.* CANDI *rides on his lap. Done up like a punk-rocker, she is significantly younger than Omar.*

Omar the Veteran wears a red beret, an eye patch, and full body camouflage. He plucks at his latex medical gloves as his miniature P.O.W. Flags trail from the wheelchair's handles.

They cackle together, startling Josie, who ducks, observing them from a dark corner.

OMAR THE VETERAN: That's what I mean! Pop 'em and drop 'em! And this asshole speaks twelve languages. Twelve! If I could do that, I wouldn't go 'round bragging about it. Snubby asshole. And he sits with me and orders drumsticks. Drumsticks, man. Not breasts or juicy thighs. Drumsticks. (*scooting forward to take the stage*) "I'll have twelve drumsticks," like a real pussy. And I cannot believe him. Not one or two. Twelve drumsticks. And he said it like that, too. I mean, I like big women. Beefy! And he had the nerve to tell her I said that!

CANDI: What?!

OMAR THE VETERAN: Oh, yeah. She asks him what I said. He says to her, "Well, he was okay with it, but I guess it wasn't great because he really likes his women big." She said that 'cause he told her. Then he tells me? Can you believe that?

CANDI: He sounds like a real catch.

OMAR THE VETERAN: (*laughs*) Oh, yeah. I hear he's not a good kisser, neither. But you like the way I kiss, don't ya'?

CANDI: I told you I did, didn't I?

OMAR THE VETERAN: You don't even remember?

CANDI: Stop bein' stupid. Tell me another war story.

OMAR THE VETERAN: I wasn't no hero, baby. They had to throw me on the plane 'cause I did not want to leave Germany. That's where I was stationed. I loved Germany. The food, the beer, the ass... but fuck Hitler! That shit was weak. Weak like I was. Yeah, baby. They had to tie me up and put me on the plane to leave Germany. Auf wiedersehen, y'know what I mean? That's how they do over there. Germany, babe. I oughta' take you to Germany.

CANDI: Hey, Omar, looks like we got company.

Omar removes his sunglasses, revealing dead, white pupils that glow in the dark.

OMAR THE VETERAN: What? Where? Hey, come out of the shadows there. You're in my tunnels. Get out here! Hey – I can see you!

JOSIE: Sorry.

OMAR THE VETERAN: We got a Bogie in the weeds here, baby.

CANDI: I'd say so. What do you want down here? You got any spare change?

OMAR THE VETERAN: Yeah. Any cash on you, man?

JOSIE: No. Sorry. I don't carry cash.

OMAR THE VETERAN: Well, to be down here in my tunnels, you gotta' pay a toll. I'm like the troll on the bridge and you're the tiny white Billy goat.

JOSIE: I'm sorry. I don't have any.

OMAR THE VETERAN: Get the hell outta' here telling me to see. I'm blind, boy! Lost my eyesight fighting in 'Nam.

CANDI: I thought you said it was over in Germany.

OMAR THE VETERAN: Yeah, that's where we fought 'em!

CANDI: I think you've got a few screws loose.

OMAR THE VETERAN: You sayin' I'm crazy?

CANDI: No. I ain't sayin' that. I'm sayin' you got a few screws loose.

OMAR THE VETERAN: Don't call me crazy, bitch!

CANDI: Don't call me a bitch, you crazy asshole!

Omar the Veteran sniffs the air in Josie's direction, waving for the Candi to disregard their bickering.

OMAR THE VETERAN: You been through heartache. I can smell it on you.

Omar leans in and takes a big whiff.

JOSIE: No. I – how can you smell something like that?

OMAR THE VETERAN: Yeah, I can smell it. Smells is free. People don't realize how much they give away with their stench. Yeah, but don't you worry. You don't have to be shy about it.

CANDI: Truly, sweetie. Omar's very good about things like that. He's very gentle. And strong. And very wise.

JOSIE: But you just called him a crazy asshole.

CANDI: He is a crazy asshole. But he knows heartache.

OMAR THE VETERAN: That's right, boy. I had a wife. And two kids. Lost all three of 'em.

JOSIE: I'm not a boy.

OMAR THE VETERAN: I can see that. Don't correct me.

CANDI: Really, honey. He hates being corrected.

JOSIE: Well, I hate being called a boy.

OMAR THE VETERAN: Oh, yeah?

JOSIE: I was always a tomboy. And once I got older, I realized I didn't know the first thing about acting romantic around a boy. Now I'm here, where I am. Alone again. So, yes. I hate being called a boy.

OMAR THE VETERAN: Yeah. You been hurt. Real recent, too. I know. I had a wife. And two kids. Long time ago. And I thought we were happy. But she wasn't–

CANDI: You see where this is going?

OMAR THE VETERAN: She cheated on me. Ran off with the kids. I trekked all over trying to find 'em. Never did. I can tell by the darkness in your eyes: you know what it feels like to have your life fall apart. It's like having PTSD. Reminds me, at least, y'know, my experience, reminded me of old Vietnam – just – a war zone, y'know? Basically, just that war zone. Palm trees and jungle birds all around and everything seems simpler than the bullshit of the First World. But then, you sit and watch big metal birds thump in and burn it down around you. And you're fine because you called in the coordinates for the air strike, but that don't make you safe. You're in the blast zone still, because there's an overzealous commander who values your life a little less than his own. We do that. All people do that. Have you noticed? Ever? They do. They certainly do. We make promises and share things intimately, but we're all awful like that. Is it inherent? It's that animal we've all got inside clawing at our hearts in the night.

JOSIE: I don't think that's true. If what you're saying is we go into something ready to hurt someone, then no, I don't think you're right.

OMAR THE VETERAN: But in the back of our heads, we know we're looking out for ourselves.

JOSIE: Everyone looks out for themselves.

OMAR THE VETERAN: Because in the end, that's all we have. We can't say a polite goodbye to the person we're trapped being. We lose parts of ourselves like bodies on a battlefield, but they breathe there, just below the surface, forever witnesses to mankind's cruelty. They linger in the dark. Beasts in the underground. Beasts in the jungle. And all these people, we're surrounded by each other, but we don't realize the self is how we're all alike. Isolated and free. Free as a bird. Birds of a feather. Apart... but together.

Omar grins at his rhyme, waiting for a response.

JOSIE: That was bad.

CANDI: Even for you.

OMAR THE VETERAN: Goddammit, now that was clever. And endearing. You gotta' give me that. I pour out my soul and manage to say something clever and you bitches scoff at it. Fuck you. Fuck off. I don't need this.

Omar wheels away angrily on his motorized wheelchair.

CANDI: What a goon.

JOSIE: It was a *really* predictable rhyme.

CANDI: Yeah. But I love him. And he's so damn cute when he gets all belligerent. (*she sighs heavily*) Y'know, I don't think he's even old enough to have been in 'Nam...

She sighs heavily and chases after Omar.

Josie trudges downstage, in the opposite direction. As she does, ROACH 1, 2 & 3 rise from a pool of opaque muck in front of her.

The three Roaches splash in the muck, all wearing clothes that were once pure and white, but are now covered in filth.

They crawl around feverishly, picking through trash. They lick and eat at empty soda cans, fast food cartons, and kitchen garbage bags.

The Roaches are lined up along the ground, sloshing through the canal between tracks, quietly working and eating.

Roach 1 reaches for Josie suddenly, splashing the trough water at her. She recoils as Cockroach 1 lunges again.

ROACH 1: Come help us. Come.

ROACH 2: Here. More to eat.

ROACH 1: Save the container!

ROACH 3: We might want it later.

ROACH 2: Here. More to eat.

ROACH 3: Save the container!

ROACH 1: We might want that later.

ROACH 2: More to eat here!

ROACH 3: Save the container!

ROACH 2: We might want it later.

ROACH 1: Keep it now. You never know when it'll be worth having around.

Their chorus makes the skin crawl. Josie covers her ears, cringing.

ROACH 3: More, please. Feed me.

ROACH 1: Save this. Tuck it away.

ROACH 2: Like memories to cherish.

ROACH 1: Like visions to store.

ROACH 3: Selfishly hoarded.

ROACH 2: Like feelings or prey.

ROACH 3: Don't ask how it tastes.

ROACH 1: I can't feel my tongue.

ROACH 3: Nothing makes sense here.

ROACH 1: Nor should it.

ROACH 2: It's done!

The Roaches crawl away into the shadows, disappearing into the ground.

Josie shudders as they go, grabbing her side as if to stifle the pain of a pinched nerve.

JOSIE: Where am I?

LIGHTS FADE.

SCENE 5

Thunder rumbles in the distance. As lightning flashes, it reveals Josie standing firmly in her spot.

Behind Josie, a lake appears. The cattails reach for a sliver of moon in the sky as fireflies dance at the water's edge.

JOSIE: When I met him, he had never seen a firefly. That was the strangest thing to me. I'd never thought anyone grew up without that experience. That's what a summer night looks like. He always smelled like some desert plant mixed with this, I don't know what you'd call it, old wooden chair? And his hands were soft. I remember liking that because my dad's were always so rough. Calloused and perpetually dirty from work. And he hadn't figured out yet how handsome he was. You could tell because he was this wild, sweet thing, but with an edge. And he lit up like a little boy the first time he saw fireflies – I don't want to talk about this. Why am I thinking this way? I was so young. We both were. I kept him from being himself. That's what people are always saying, isn't it? It's what he said. And he says now he doesn't mean it. That we should work things out. But I said that first. I went there first. And he ignored it. I believe he tried not to hurt me. But that's been the scariest thing about this. And I don't think he knows it. I hope he never will. When you get dangerously close to someone, you can feel them falling out of love with you. People

JOSIE (cont.): don't realize that. When you're really truly close to someone, you feel them slip away. Slowly. Steadily. Like rain falling on a summer evening. They tiptoe around, trying not to hurt you, thinking you don't see them welling up, ready to let themselves slip down the gutter. I went out to see him – to win him back. But I sat in the room with those girls. His new friends. His new, temporary friends. I'd never been so insecure about him keeping female friends. Never had that worry with him. Because I remember how he'd look at me. And I always thought I'd be the one to hurt him. Worried that I wasn't good for him. So, I didn't understand feeling that way there. In that moment, surrounded by people he'd only known for four weeks, I backed away. I watched him tease them like some third grader who didn't understand his feelings. And I stood there, trying to blend in. Trying to be one of the girls he was balancing in his game. He hadn't been that part of himself for nearly six years. When we first met. And I knew he was better off. Because if that person can leave you behind in favor of near-strangers, and that person – that same person – promised you they'd never leave you behind, then you have to step back. I know I can't tell him this now. Because now he's convinced he's back. But I'm trapped here, and I don't want to move from this spot because something here smells like that firewood cloud that belongs to the person I loved. The person who amputated part of himself from my heart. I'm better off here. Between. Lost in those moments. He can't take those from me. And

JOSIE (cont.): they're still good, so I'll hold onto them. I don't know what else to do. In the end, I'm the only one I was sharing them with anyway. I'm being punished. If I knew who I was, I'd apologize. That's fine. I'll take that. But everything is clouded, like a smoky room. Faulty wiring. I don't want to listen to myself trying to make this decision.

The PASTOR shuffles in, appearing high on a platform above Josie. He looks like a medieval monk wearing a tunic made of comic book pages. He clutches a copy of 'The Necronomicon.'

He has an accent that suggests he comes from some far-off corner of the world, but with all the flare befitting a fifteen-year-old dungeon master.

PASTOR: Consider the lilies of the valley: they fall every season under the shadow of winter winds, dropping like undergarments on prom night. Nothing is sacred, as the great god Azathoth perpetuates chaos from his nucleic positioning at the center of our precious universe. From him, let all animal urges boil over. Let us embrace the apes from whence we came. This is why even the happiest of committed persons will always look lustfully at another. The chaos beneath the surface of our skin is woven into the fabric of our DNA.

JOSIE: But I know he loves me...

PASTOR: We, the people, are despicable creatures capable of the worst exploitations imaginable. Embrace it. Don't think about it. Find within you

PASTOR (cont.): the Alpha – the pack leader. Forget not the baboons who represent the part of man that still hasn't climbed down from the trees. Do not forget that we are animals. All of us.

JOSIE: Then I should forgive him. That's what I can give. I don't know which life to choose. I wanted to be married. I did. I wanted to keep telling the same story. How can I say that, though, if I don't go back?

PASTOR: When I was a boy, I watched a baboon troop at the zoo restructure itself. There was a smart baboon of average size who eventually outsmarted the big, butch baboon troop leader. And I connected with that baboon. Cheered for him, even. He was tinier and he had to outsmart that big, macho leader. Because I want to puff up my chest and protect my own. I want to stick out my big blue ass and shove it in someone else's way even though I know they've got a blue ass twice the size of my head! I don't care! And the baboon... he was smart. And he stuck his blue ass in there with confidence!

JOSIE: I can't go back... he doesn't need me. Did I really cheat us out of our youth? (*shaking her head*) I don't know. It wasn't a bad time... was it?

PASTOR: I feel the urge to growl and stomp and show my big blue ass to the other man, so he sees it and says to himself, "Ah, yes. This baboon: his smart ass is better." And one day, it is my hope that we will all accept this in ourselves and let ourselves be swept away by the chaos.

Beneath the Pastor, BOXER 1 *and* BOXER 2 *emerge from the shadows with hairy, ape-like forearms and bruised, swollen faces. They slug each other mercilessly.*

The LAUGHING GIRL *sits in a corner, laughing as the Boxers pummel each other. She reacts to the other characters on stage, but they do not react to her.*

Josie is drawn to them all, but shrieks as they tackle each other to the ground, wriggling like infants. It is unclear if they are in pain or enjoying their experience. Blood spills from the Pastor's feet onto the fighting men.

JOSIE: I'm being punished. Here between decisions. I'll take that. If I knew who I was, I'd apologize to myself. But I don't want to listen to myself trying to make this decision.

The subway car rolls downstage, splitting open. It spews Josie's memories everywhere. Picture frames shatter, photos burn. Mementos rain down from the heavens.

Josie collapses as madness sets in.

BLACKOUT.

SCENE 6

The subway car is tattered, and the Boxers' blood spatters glow red with molten fury in the rocky tunnel. Is this a channel under Manhattan, or the mouth to Hell?

Lights up on THOMAS *downstage. He should be significantly taller than Josie, awkward but endearing, and unaware of his good looks. This is Josie's estranged husband, and he looks a lot like Oliver the note thief.*

THOMAS: Last night, I heard cicadas chirping through my heater. My electric heater out in Queens.

JOSIE: Is that where you're at now?

THOMAS: Yeah. At a buddy's. You don't know her – she was on my last gig. Helped backstage.

JOSIE: Oh.

THOMAS: But. So... last night I was hearing the cicadas. In my heater. And I felt like my nervous system was floating gently on a breeze. Six feet above my bed. Like I had managed to propel myself back into a memory. Nothing special either, but a regular night lying in my bed as a kid. In the summer. And I thought maybe I'd die in my sleep right then and there. Just float on. But a hand draped itself across my chest. Flesh on flesh... And it was comforting... and it was asking me to stay. Without any force. Like it was truly my choice. And requests like those should be honored.

JOSIE: Do you remember that history class we took together: the Wild American West? Such a weird, randomly specific history class. I thought it would be a rad topic. And you said it'd be an easy A, since it was just a recap of history you grew up learning?

THOMAS: I remember the class. Did I really say that?

JOSIE: Yeah. And you got a C.

THOMAS: I remember the C.

JOSIE: One of the lectures still pops up in my head. It was a really rainy day – one of the ones you skipped – I remember leaving you in bed, still wrapped up in the sheets. That day we talked about the concept of the decaying West. The idea was – or *is* – that, as technology and populations increased during the twentieth century, the wild has gotten worn out of the West. Think about that. In our own country, there's a way of life just dying. And it's not just here. It happens everywhere. And then you think, the East had to decay first. The Industrial Revolution took the East first. People used to rough it in North Carolina and Virginia and Pennsylvania. That way of life is gone, too. When I met you and started traveling out there, that affected me. And I fell in love with it. It was so simple and beautiful and honest. And I wanted it. I grabbed hold of it and tried to romanticize it for myself. Those snow-capped mountains staggering across the wide-open sky like a line of hairy old men at the pharmacy. Trees so wise, you expect them to shake the snow from their branches and start

41

JOSIE (cont.): telling you stories. And rocks so bright you start looking for the straps to Mother Nature's sundress. It was never mine. And I'm hurting because you make me feel like the West crumbled just a little more in my grip because I held on too tight...

Thomas may look at Josie from here on, but she does not respond or react in a way that acknowledges his physical presence on stage.

THOMAS: It's unfair. I don't love like that. I couldn't stand by like you do and just let opportunities pass by because I'm supposed to stay put and love someone.

JOSIE: People love in different ways.

THOMAS: But shouldn't I be crazy about you?

JOSIE: Different people are crazy in different ways.

THOMAS: I just – I don't think I was happy when we were together.

JOSIE: And I thought we were happy.

THOMAS: But I told you I wasn't.

JOSIE: And I told you when I wasn't, too. But I always came back. Just cloudy days. Everyone has cloudy days. I've been telling you that since we met. People have each other for help catching glimpses of sunlight. Two heads are better than one. That's why we love... no matter how we love or who we love.

THOMAS: I never felt like I gave you much light on your cloudy days.

JOSIE: Then why am I the one in this position? (*Thomas has no answer. Josie waits a beat.*) Did you know she tried to warn me it was coming?

THOMAS: Who?

JOSIE: Jane. Good, sweet, perfect Jane.

THOMAS: Hey – don't. Please?

JOSIE: What? She was right. I wouldn't speak ill of Miss Perfect–

THOMAS: Stop–

JOSIE: (*mock-swooning*) The one who got away. (*then, severely*) She's so average, Tom–

THOMAS: Jo–

JOSIE: Oh, what? She was as exciting as a wet plaid dish cloth!

THOMAS: Jo! (*Josie recoils in shame*) She's grounded. She's comfortable with herself and her accomplishments.

JOSIE: I'm sorry. I'm thankful for her, I guess. At least she bought me time to try and get you back. Even if she did have you pleading outside her door. She tried to stay out of our way. She respected what we had. Even if she didn't get it. She did have the nerve to tell me she'd experienced something similar and that I'd be okay. I'm still not certain of that. And not thrilled with her act. The older, wiser girl who's already seen it all. She told me – the night we were all out – I pulled her aside to thank her for staying out of it – and she told me I'd be okay. That she'd lost someone close, too.

JOSIE (cont.): She said she didn't think our love – yours and mine – was as mature as the love she'd had for her person.

THOMAS: Huh. Okay, that's annoying, I guess, but she was trying to be nice. That's how she is—

JOSIE: No. No. It's bullshit. Why can't you get defensive about us? You immediately defend her, but you've known her for a fraction of a year. Our love isn't as mature? That doesn't make you just a little indignant? She'd known you for a month – your *worst* month, as far as our relationship goes. Plus, you know it's bullshit, Mister 'love is love.' How many times have you thrown that at me during this fucking commitment tantrum of yours? But you're not wrong. Love just *is*. It's as mature as the people who are in it. But it's still love. We all have that capacity.

THOMAS: She had no right. She was wrong.

JOSIE: Three times, Tom. Right in a row.

THOMAS: Please—

Now Josie can acknowledge Thomas's physical presence in the same space as her. Whether or not this is an apparition generated by Josie, she is convinced it's playing out for her.

JOSIE: No. I stood by you for that. I have no idea why I did. But that counts for something. And no one knows because I don't tell people that. I won't tell people any of that because I know you. I care about you. And I don't want anyone to think differently of you. You're a good person. You are. And I do love you… did. I really did. But I

JOSIE (cont.): just can't anymore. I know you had a bad time, too. It makes me sad because I couldn't fix it for you. But I'm only so strong. Everyone is only so strong. I've always wanted to be that strong, loving type. Motherly and stern and grounded and quiet, but beautiful and sweet and gentle and understanding. Like a dogwood tree watching over a flower garden. The one who stands by, even if her husband falters. Because she can't help herself; she loves him. But I lost myself in the process. Because you were such a big part of me.

THOMAS: We're never going to get past it, though, if you can't forgive me.

JOSIE: I do forgive you. But forgetting is different. I lost hold of who I was. I broke. I broke when our trust broke. Remember that candy dish I had? I got it from my great-grandmother after she passed away – just before you and I started dating – and it's all I wanted to remember her by. Because there was always candy in the dish sitting out on the coffee table when I'd go see her. Remember? We had your birthday party at the apartment when we first moved to the city, and your buddy was there high on God-knows-what. He dropped a mug while he was digging through our cupboards, and it shot my dish right off the counter and cracked it into five or six pieces. And I just cried the second it cracked off the floor. You tried so hard to fix it for me, but all those little pieces- the shards we swept into the trash – they were all lost. And you said we wouldn't be able to see the cracks. But we could. I could.

THOMAS: At least you still have it.

JOSIE: I don't. I threw it away.

THOMAS: But you loved that!

JOSIE: After that happened, I just saw the cracks. All those hairline fractures. I didn't see my great-grandmother's dish anymore.

THOMAS: That's so close-minded! It's still the same dish!

JOSIE: No. Because my great-grandmother took care of it for a century

THOMAS: That's an exaggeration.

JOSIE: No, it isn't. She lived until she was ninety-nine, and the dish was a gift to her from *her* grandmother. It's not an exaggeration! By the time I got it and your stupid friend broke it, the thing had been around for a century. Okay?

THOMAS: *Okay...*

JOSIE: *(after a beat)* And all through college, I managed to take care of it. I couldn't take care of things with you. And that's what I saw when I looked at that dish with all those cracks in it.

THOMAS: It was just a thing. Things aren't perfect. They get used.

JOSIE: You're so rough with everything – your whole family is. I don't just want to replace my things when they break. Some things are worth saving.

THOMAS: That's so stupid! Things are just things! They're made to be used and run their course–

JOSIE: I don't want a cracked fucking candy dish! Okay?

THOMAS: Okay! (*beat*) Okay... You seem more like yourself without me. You look more comfortable with yourself.

JOSIE: No. Don't decide that for me. You don't get to decide that for me. Because I feel exactly the opposite. (*beat*) What about you? Are you happy now?

THOMAS: I don't know.

JOSIE: No one's holding you back now.

THOMAS: I'm lonely. I get lonely. I don't want accountability for anyone but me. That feels like freedom. And some of the people I've met, they're fine, but... they're – I don't know – two-dimensional?

JOSIE: Oh, fuck off.

THOMAS: What?

JOSIE: Of course they're two-dimensional, Tom! You've only known these people for a month or a few weeks or maybe even less. That's not long enough to get to know someone. Do you not get that? (*beat*) Who are you meeting?

THOMAS: Just friends. I'm meeting friends. I'm trying to figure out how to be friends with people. Because I can't just stop believing in love. And that's what's happening; I don't believe in love anymore. At least, I don't think I do. I think we get tied up and tied down, but all we really want is physical comfort. It just feels like humans overcomplicate everything, y'know? And I'm just

THOMAS (cont.): so sick of everything always being so fucking complicated.

JOSIE: That's just *life*, Tom. We have to grow up and manage our own lives. There is no alternative. It's the commitment thrust on all of us the second we're born. Time just... keeps on slippin'.

THOMAS: (*laughing at her reference*) Yeah. (*beat*) I'm sorry for all of it. For what it's worth, I haven't been as comfortable with another person. I'm not thinking about what might happen if you come back, because I know you aren't. Neither is the person I was. Or the person you were. That's why I need you to make this decision.

JOSIE: It's not fair to ask me to do that.

THOMAS: Get to the front of the train.

Thomas disappears.

JOSIE: I'm trying. Tom? Tom! (beat) Wait!

Her voice echoes back to her.

SCENE 7

JOSIE *stands onstage alone, stuck in the spot where Tom left her.*

UNCLE BOB *lumbers in. His work boots are so big, he has to walk around them. He's a walking stereotype of 'working class,' from the coveralls and hard hat down to the Brooklyn accent.*

Bob runs up to Josie and hugs her.

JOSIE: Uncle Bob? What're you doing here?

UNCLE BOB: Who? What're you sayin'? Ah, forget about it. I'm just here to say I'm sorry. I think this is my fault.

JOSIE: What's your fault?

UNCLE BOB: The whole thing, even the explosion.

JOSIE: There was an explosion?

UNCLE BOB: Yeah and... look, the thing is, I think I may have been able to prevent it. But I didn't. And I don't know if you're alive or dead because I don't know if I am or not, but I'm sorry. If you're dead. I'm sorry because maybe I could have done something to stop it.

JOSIE: I don't understand what you're trying to say.

UNCLE BOB: I'm an observant guy, is what I guess I'm trying to say. I'm not racist, but I listen to stereotypes, y'know? There's value in them

UNCLE BOB (cont.): because they come from somewhere. No. I don't mean that. That sounds ridiculous.

JOSIE: Yes. And extremely racist.

UNCLE BOB: Yeah. No. I try to be open-minded while being aware of my surroundings, is what I'm really sayin' here. But listen! So, I'm on the train car at the very front, and right around Jay Street this guy gets on. He's dressed in a nice sweater. Well, it's this heinous prep school big stripes thing in navy and green. Like a Gap ad or – or a rugby jersey! You ever see those ugly things? Yeah. So, he's dressed decent, depending on your sense of fashion. But y'know, he's not a slob, okay? But he's got this big bushy beard and a tangerine-colored turban on. And my first thought is how jittery he is. He gets on, but he's not sitting down. Then he walks to a seat and-and he sits, then jumps right up again. And he's playing with his phone and looks distressed and then he's bowing his head like he's praying. And y'know, I lived through all that media garbage propaganda post-nine-eleven, and in the whitest part of my fuckin' brain I'm thinking, 'Oh, shit! This guy's a terrorist! He's got to be.' But I immediately say, 'Hey Bob, that's racist.' Then I'm thinking, 'No, he's wearing those, what are they, those Hindi turbans. That's Indian. It looks like the ones in that Wes Anderson movie about the Orient Express or whatever. And those guys wear those and they're Indian. So, I'm at ease there for a sec, but this guy is white.

JOSIE: He was a white guy?

UNCLE BOB: Yeah. At least, I think so. I guess I shouldn't assume. But he looked pretty white. But with a Hindi turban and stuff. And hey, we come in many shapes and sizes, right? So, why should I judge this guy? Y'know? This guy, maybe he's, uh – British! They're the white people who made a mess over there, right?

JOSIE: Yes.

UNCLE BOB: So, maybe he grew up over there because his British family is still over there, and he's over here now. How am I supposed to know? Not my business, right? That's respectful thinking, right?

JOSIE: Yeah.

UNCLE BOB: Yeah, okay. I'm glad we agree. Yeah, so, where was I? He's a white guy in a Hindi turban and all. And that's fine. But what gets to me is he's staring people down. And the whites of his eyes are all pink. So, I'm thinking he's on something for sure. Then he's fidgeting with his fucking phone and staring down these Chinese tourists and bowing his head again and again. And I'm getting anxious 'cause I'm in close quarters with this guy and the train is just crawling and on top of it all I'm confused *and* I'm a racist! I practically plow through the doors at the next stop, and I switched train cars. And we're stuck in this goddamn tunnel now and all I can think is, 'Am I a bad person?' But I'm also thinking, 'Shit, what if that guy was the reason for the explosion? And my observation could've

UNCLE BOB (cont.): saved lives!' Like those ads: If you see something, say something. I mean, Jesus, we're under water! I can't even hold my breath that long! I don't wanna' go out that way: sucking in a lung full of water!

Uncle Bob's voice crescendos into a mad shriek.

JOSIE: Uncle Bob!? Calm down!

UNCLE BOB: Huh? Oh, sure. Don't worry about me. I don't even know where we are. And try not to shout so much, Josie. Yikes.

JOSIE: We're underground. The train was derailed.

UNCLE BOB: No, it exploded.

JOSIE: There was no explosion. You're just in a state of trauma.

UNCLE BOB: No. I don't want you to think that. Don't think that!

JOSIE: I already do. But that's okay. It's perfectly natural. We're human – we have emotional reactions to things. Sometimes for better, sometimes for worse.

UNCLE BOB: Shit. That's deep.

JOSIE: Yeah.

They sit in silence for a moment.

UNCLE BOB: Hey, how's Timmy?

JOSIE: Who?

UNCLE BOB: Your husband?

JOSIE: Tommy. He goes by Thomas now.

UNCLE BOB: Sounds a little uppity.

JOSIE: It sounds super fucking pretentious.

UNCLE BOB: Whoa, hey – I struck a chord, huh?

JOSIE: Yeah. Yeah, things aren't great between us.

UNCLE BOB: Well, there's nothing you can't work through together.

JOSIE: You know how Aunt Kelly left you?

UNCLE BOB: Oh... Oh! Oh, Josie, sweetie, I'm sorry. I'm so sorry.

He wraps her up in a big hug. After a moment, he breaks the hug and leans over so they're face-to-face.

UNCLE BOB: Listen, I want you to remember something. Hold onto it, because you're gonna' need it.

JOSIE: (*meeting his gaze*): What's that?

UNCLE BOB: It's not you. What he's doing – it's not because of you. I mean, I'm sure your partnership has its frustrations and challenges, and familiarity does breed contempt, like they say, but what I mean is: this is his problem. There's nothing wrong with you. You're a hell of a catch! Smart, pretty – not too girly – y'know, you're a well-rounded person. A Renaissance Woman! And I just think you're the bee's knees.

JOSIE: (*fighting tears*) Thanks, Uncle Bob. That's... I appreciate that.

UNCLE BOB: And I mean it! Every word. It's the truth, and it's what I wish someone had been able to

UNCLE BOB (cont.): tell me, y'know? Yeah, Aunt Kelly, she… I don't wanna' speak ill, she's your cousin's mother, but that woman – sheesh. We went on trips as much as I could manage, I always tried to, uh, keep the romance fresh, but I work, too. I work fifty, sometimes sixty hours a week. So, I'm tuned out a lot, and she was lonely. Plain and simple. She let herself feel abandoned, instead of focusing on those positives. There's no sense to it. No sense, just self. And if you don't see it coming, (*he claps his hands or smacks something*) Bang! It hits you like an Express Train heading uptown at rush hour. (*anxiety creeps back in – he looks around warily*) Where are we?

JOSIE: In the subway tunnels. Underground.

UNCLE BOB: Where are we timewise?

JOSIE: The train's been down for, I don't know- an hour? Maybe just under?

UNCLE BOB: I'm so confused. See, I've been to the beginning, and I definitely know how things end: How they're supposed to end. For me. But I'm in the middle and I don't know whether or not I should be making any assessments or decisions, or anything like that. Because I can't tell anymore how much it'll affect the beginning and the end. I don't want the middle to, uh, suck… if you will. But then I think, "Maybe the middle is supposed to suck, and the end will come as slowly as it wants." Who knows if I'll touch the ethereal plain? Maybe I'm trapped here. In between stations. Hell, in between boroughs. Underwater. In a tube in the ground. Fuckin' crazy, right?

JOSIE: (*as if to confirm that he most certainly is*) Yeah. Fuckin' crazy.

UNCLE BOB: Yeah. I gotta get back to the front of the train.

He runs off stage right.

JOSIE: (*shouting after Bob*) But you were heading towards the back. I'm heading to the front!

Uncle Bob continues running, calling back to her as he goes, but not correcting course.

UNCLE BOB: Shit! I always do that!

BLACKOUT.

SCENE 8

In the dark, the LAUGHING GIRL *cackles.*

LIGHTS UP.

OLIVER *wanders out of the shadows. His clothing is tattered and dirty, his body bruised and battered, but his glasses are inexplicably untouched.*

The Laughing Girl lurks in a corner opposite the action, laughing in her trance.

JOSIE: *(under her breath)* You. *(shouting)* Hey, Oliver! Where's my note?

He doesn't respond. Josie lunges for him, grabbing his arm. He turns and they lock eyes, but Josie recoils.

OLIVER: No. Sorry. Wrong person.

JOSIE: Oh.

It is definitely Oliver. There should be no question that this is the same man from Scene 1.

JOSIE: Wait. No, I want my letter back. You have my letter. You stole it.

OLIVER: I don't have a letter and I don't steal.

JOSIE: Prove it!

OLIVER: How?

JOSIE: I don't know... Check your pockets! Turn them inside out and everything.

Oliver obliges and pats himself down, turning his pants pockets inside out.

OLIVER: Nothing. See?

JOSIE: Are you sure?

OLIVER: I am most definitely sure. You've got me mistaken for someone else. I guarantee it.

JOSIE: What's your name?

OLIVER: Well, that is difficult. I'm not entirely sure I remember. But it's got a rolling vowel sound at the beginning. The sound that suggests it encompasses a lot and calls forth rolling hills.

JOSIE: Like an O, maybe?

OLIVER: Yes. Oh. Oooooh. Yes, I think that's it.

JOSIE: Are you coming from the train?

OLIVER: What train?

JOSIE: The subway. I'm trying to get to the end of the tunnel – er – the front of the train, technically.

OLIVER: The light.

JOSIE: What light?

OLIVER: The light at the end of the tunnel? It's an expression about death.

JOSIE: Yeah, I'm familiar with the expression.

OLIVER: May I ask a rather personal question?

JOSIE: I can't guarantee I'll answer.

OLIVER: Please do. I'm a bit concerned about what it is I'm doing.

JOSIE: Okay... I'm not following you. At all.

OLIVER: Do you ever tune into your habits and realize how animalistic you're being? All of us, we all have little things. I drink these health shakes now. I never did, but I do now. With nuts. And ginger. And sometimes I don't get the portions right, so I end up chewing some of it. I don't mind at all. I kind of like the texture. Like I'm communing with my mouth. But when I do it out in public, like on the subway, I feel like a rabbit chewing clover, and I wonder if other people see me and think the same thing. I'm pretty sure my nose wiggles the same way and my cheeks do sometimes feel chubbier than they are.

JOSIE: I had friends who had rabbits growing up. I thought the rabbits were really sweet and cute and I wanted one all to myself. But that would always go away immediately when the friend would say I couldn't pet the rabbit because they don't like to be held. What's the point of having a fuzzy little thing of your own if it doesn't want to be held? I don't like boys like that, either. Well, men, I guess. When they don't want to be touched. Except for sex. Just like the damn rabbits. Can't we just hold each other?

OLIVER: I agree with you. Or at least I think I do. And I'm not making a pass at you, either. Truly. I'm not even sure if my agreeing with you is how I'm supposed to feel. Because I can't quite remember who I'm supposed to be. Perhaps I *am* a rabbit? *The* rabbit! The white rabbit. I do feel very late, indeed. (*he pats himself down*) Where's my pocket

OLIVER (cont.): watch? (*thinking hard*) I don't have a pocket watch!

JOSIE: Do you remember hiding a letter? Putting it somewhere?

OLIVER: I'm sorry? Was that me?

JOSIE: Yes. I'm certain of it. You were trying to find your initials carved into the seats of the subway–

OLIVER: (*nodding excitedly*) Yes! I just want to sit with it for a while! Yes! Try to take it all in again. Remember her smell. Her hair and her laugh. I can remember her name: Josie Richter. But she's faceless.

Josie freezes.

JOSIE: No. That's my name. You just used my name.

OLIVER: (*unfazed*) But she's faceless. I never thought I'd do that. We carved out a place – our place – here on a train car. A little place in time. A way to be remembered by strangers. But if that's what I was doing...

Oliver wanders upstage left, towards the mouth of Hell.

JOSIE: What the hell are you doing?

Josie freezes.

Oliver crosses upstage to the Mouth of Hell in darkness, where he peels away his clothing and skin to reveal THOMAS underneath it all. He pulls out a pocket watch and winds it noisily.

THOMAS: Hold that thought.

Thomas puts some of his Oliver clothes back on.

Josie jumps aside as a metal door groans open and HELEN *from Scene 1 enters. She floats upstage to a couch and reclining chair, both of which look and feel like something that should have been burned and buried when the 1960s ended.*

She switches on a TV. The screen faces upstage, but the noises coming from the TV are undoubtedly sexual. Grunting, moaning, and even the sick wet smack of moist flesh.

Thomas pulls Josie's note from his breast pocket – the same note Oliver stole.

JOSIE: That belongs to me.

Thomas/Oliver ignores her. He hands Helen the note.

THOMAS: I thought we were good?

HELEN: You said it wouldn't happen again. You promised.

THOMAS: And you said we were good.

HELEN: Yeah, well, I guess we're not.

THOMAS: It was just a kiss! A kiss and a little hand-play. And then I cut it off. I shut it down. It's nothing like – like…

HELEN: Like when we were young? Is that what you want to say? Except it is, isn't it? Every few years, this seems to happen. Sometimes it lasts longer than others, but I'm always waiting for the crash. So here it is. Again.

THOMAS: And here I am.

Josie storms upstage. First, she snatches the letter from Thomas. Then, she swats at the television until she manages to shut it off, killing the pornographic sounds.

JOSIE: What's your point, Tom?

In a tantrum, Thomas tears off the Oliver suit. As he does, Helen shudders, breaking into quiet sobs.

THOMAS: C'mon, my scene was just getting started! Don't be weird!

JOSIE: I'm not being weird! Why does everyone always fucking say that? I'm just being myself. I've been more myself than you have. I'm sick of being told how to think. That's all you do. You tell me how to think. And I don't know who to ignore: you, or me. But I can never get input that's not contradictory. Like jamming the wrong puzzle pieces into one of those insanely complicated jigsaws. Have you ever tried to start in the middle of the picture? It makes no sense, but that's how you insist we do it every fucking time! There's no structure.

THOMAS: There doesn't need to be structure. You've got to let go of that.

JOSIE: No. No. There does need to be structure. For me, there needs to be structure, okay? I want the border on a puzzle taken care of first, especially one that's over a thousand pieces! Structure is not a bad thing for everyone. Not for me. It helps me. I function better with it... Oh, God. That's why I was the happy one, isn't it? That's why...

During her speech, Thomas gets emotional. He should most certainly be fighting tears by the time he speaks.

THOMAS: I'm sorry. I hurt you. There are still a lot more good memories. I just – I couldn't focus on them. I am now. If you come home, I am focusing on those things.

Josie reaches to hug him. She stops. He looks at her, tears running down his face. She takes a step back.

THOMAS: Is this it?

JOSIE: What?

THOMAS: Is this where you leave?

JOSIE: Yeah... yes. Yes, it definitely is.

THOMAS: I'll never see you again. If you go, that's it. I've got to move on.

JOSIE: I know.

THOMAS: I'm sorry.

JOSIE: I can't–

THOMAS: Please know how sorry I am.

JOSIE: I do. And some day, I'll be able to forgive you. But I can't right now. I don't recognize you anymore. I don't recognize us. And you're right; I'm not happy. You don't make me happy. But I still care about you. As a human. As someone I was friends with. I do care. But I don't like who we've become.

THOMAS: If you cared, you'd come back!

JOSIE: That's not fair.

THOMAS: You're quitting. Just like you always do. Please. Come make this work with me. You say all these things. You say you care about me, and you forgive me. But here we are. I'm heading home. Where are you heading? What are you doing? Come home. Please. I love you. I fucked up, and I just want to make it right. Come home! Please?

JOSIE: I'm never coming home.

The red light in the tunnel intensifies and distorted silhouettes drag Thomas away.

Josie cries as they are separated, but she also does nothing to stop it.

BLACKOUT.

SCENE 9

LIGHTS UP SLOWLY.

The MOLE PEOPLE *close in around Josie. They move with a sense of ownership. This is their world and others are not welcome.*

They are haggard, their faces distorted. With big, opaque eyes and rubbery faces, they look like monsters from an old 1950's B-Movie. They all wear various MTA uniforms covered in soot and mud and grime.

Some wear hard hats and coveralls, others wear conductor garb.

They move around in a group, choreographed. Although they seem silent, there is a shrill chirping sound that accompanies their movement. Perhaps they sound like rats... or is that a banjo? Whatever the noise, it is unsettling.

JOSIE: Stop! Just, please stop! You can't keep me down here. I'm drowning in my past and all I wanted to do today was go see my husband – ex-husband! I don't know! I don't know what to call him, I don't know if I want to see his face. But I do know that in the last six months, my life has gone to complete shit, and the last thing I want is to be trapped down here in this goddamned tunnel with you people! I'm moving on. This was my day to start shoveling the shit in someone else's path. Anyone! I don't care who. Just not mine. My path is already covered in heaps of shit. So, don't tell

JOSIE (cont.): me to calm down. Don't tell me you fuckers are sorry for the inconvenience. I'm supposed to be uptown, severing ties so that I can finally face the fact that I'm about to be twenty-six and divorced. Okay? Get the fuck out of my way!

The mole people stop her.

JOSIE: Move! I said move! Don't push me out of the way like some adolescent who doesn't know her place. I know where I belong. I finally know where I belong and I'm not moving for anyone. I'm done being the nice one! The people-pleaser! Under a microscope, changing the fibers of my being in order to keep someone else happy. I legitimately don't care. I don't care what people think anymore! I have nothing left to lose! Except my memories, and believe me, there are plenty of those I'd like you to just suck right out of my brain.

MOLE PERSON 1: We will not harm you, but you cannot go any further.

MOLE PERSON 2: We understand your pain.

JOSIE: How? What have you got, huh? A tunnel of dirt? Clothes covered in filth that clings to you like maggots to a carcass. You're subterranean beings. You literally live beneath the rest of us. In rags. That's what this is. A colony of sub-humans with no lives. You don't get to be human and live outside of society like this. And shun others if they come across you. I've heard about you. I didn't believe you existed, but I've heard of you.

JOSIE (cont.): They say no one comes in or out of your little caverns. That you're animals.

MOLE PERSON 1: And do we appear as such to you?

JOSIE: Yes! Yes, you do!

MOLE PERSON 2: We have not yet shunned you. Or devoured your flesh. Or accused you of being less than us.

JOSIE: You said I couldn't go home.

MOLE PERSON 1: And in your anger, you confirmed it.

JOSIE: Confirmed what?

MOLE PERSON 1: That you can't go home. You can't go home without knowing what you want, of course. What do you want?

JOSIE: I want to get out of these caves. I want to get to the surface. I'd even go back to the train! Where's the train?

MOLE PERSON 2: Yours was the last train home.

JOSIE: The trains run all the time, so that's not true.

MOLE PERSON 1: There are no more trains home. You got off the last one. That was the last train home.

JOSIE: Christ, just stop! Make this nightmare end. Stop the weirdness and the chanting and all of it! Stop it! I want you to stop!

MOLE PERSON 2: Beyond that, what do you want?

JOSIE: I don't know! What kind of question is that?

MOLE PERSON 1: You must. You must always know what you want.

JOSIE: I have nothing left! I have no direction. Hell, I don't even have a place to stay tonight.

MOLE PERSON 2: Stay here.

JOSIE: In a dirty underground tunnel?

MOLE PERSON 1: It could be worse. You have no home!

JOSIE: Maybe not here. But don't I always have a home? Isn't that what they say? (*beat*) No. That's not home. I have no home.

MOLE PERSON 1: If you have no home, where are you headed?

JOSIE: Home.

MOLE PERSON 2: That cannot be.

MOLE PERSON 1: You're contradicting yourself.

JOSIE: No. I know what I'm saying. Just let me finish. It was my home. It's not anymore. I'm not going back.

MOLE PERSON 1: But you're going back now.

MOLE PERSON 2: Yes. You just said so.

JOSIE: You're not understanding me.

MOLE PERSON 1: We understand perfectly. You seem to be very confused.

JOSIE: I know what I'm doing!

MOLE PERSON 1: No. You have to know what you want in order to know what you're doing. It's the order of things. You're warned very early, too.

MOLE PERSON 2: Plenty of notice. Figure out what you want.

JOSIE: Stop telling me no! I don't know what I want.

MOLE PERSON 1: You must.

JOSIE: That doesn't change my answer! I don't know what I want. If that's what you want from me, you're not getting it. I'm trying to act like I know what I'm doing. See, you've got me confused. I didn't do this myself. I know what I'm doing. But I don't know what I want. I want too many things. I would've wanted whatever made him happy!

MOLE PERSON 2: That boy? No, he looked sad.

MOLE PERSON 1: You certainly didn't seem to make him happy.

JOSIE: (*deflated*) Really?

The mole people start chanting. They are gradually joined by more and more voices of the unseen underground denizens who remain in the shadows.

MOLE PEOPLE: What do you want? What do you want? What do you want? What do you want?

They continue to chant, and the four mole people who are visible circle around her, closing in like sharks around a carcass.

JOSIE: (*feebly*) I don't know. I don't know. I don't know!

The Mole People are unrelenting, continuing their chant. Josie drops to her knees in the dirt. She sobs, reduced to the fetal position.

The blackness closes in on Josie, engulfing the mole people and isolating her. The chanting stops as she sobs in her solitary light.

BLACKOUT.

JOSIE & HELEN: Can you hear me?

In the darkness, a thin crack of light illuminates Josie's unconscious body. The light intensifies, revealing a FIREFIGHTER *leaning over Josie.*

The Firefighter is Helen.

FIREFIGHTER: Miss? Can you hear me?

Josie woozily nods.

FIREFIGHTER: Okay? Are you okay?

Josie nods again.

FIREFIGHTER: I'm here to help. You're gonna' be okay. We'll get you back home.

Josie looks at the Firefighter, then collapses.

BLACKOUT.

END

WINZEK

ABOUT THE PLAYWRIGHT

Author & entertainer Brent Winzek was born and raised in the hills of Pittsburgh, Pennsylvania, where everyone knew him as the resident *Jurassic Park* aficionado. He attained a Bachelor of Arts in Film Production and a Master of Arts in Theater from Bowling Green State University in Ohio before moving to New York City where he worked in the TV & film, Broadway, Off-Broadway, and academic circles of entertainment. He continues to write & produce strange original work from deep within a forested hovel alongside his wife and critters.

To explore his other projects, visit
spacecadetsstudios.com